Overqualified.

Joey Comeau

ECW Press

overqualified

Published by ECW Press, 2120 Queen Street East, Suite 200,
Toronto, Ontario, Canada M4E 1E2 / 416.694.3348 / info@ecwpress.com

LIBRARY AND ARCHIVES CANADA CATALOGUING IN PUBLICATION

Comeau, Joey, 1980–
Overqualified / Joey Comeau.

ISBN-13: 978-1-55022-858-8
ISBN-10: 1-55022-858-7

I. Title.

PS8605.O537O94 2009   C813'.6   C2008-905429-6

Editor for the press: Michael Holmes
Cover images: Joey Comeau (front); Russell McBride / iStockPhoto (back)
Production: Rachel Ironstone
Printing: Coach House   4 5

This book is set in Janson and Love Letter.

The publication of *Overqualified* has been generously supported by
the Canada Council for the Arts, which last year invested $20.1 million in
writing and publishing throughout Canada, by the Ontario Arts Council, by the
Government of Ontario through Ontario Book Publishing Tax Credit, by the OMDC
Book Fund, an initiative of the Ontario Media Development Corporation,
and by the Government of Canada through the Book Publishing
Industry Development Program (BPIDP).

Canada Council   Conseil des Arts   Canada   ONTARIO ARTS COUNCIL
for the Arts   du Canada   CONSEIL DES ARTS DE L'ONTARIO

PRINTED AND BOUND IN CANADA

MISFIT

ECW PRESS
ecwpress.com